Edith Nesbit

A Pomander of Verse

Edith Nesbit

A Pomander of Verse

ISBN/EAN: 9783337737818

Printed in Europe, USA, Canada, Australia, Japan

Cover: Foto ©Andreas Hilbeck / pixelio.de

More available books at **www.hansebooks.com**

 POMANDER
OF VERSE

BY
E. NESBIT

LONDON: JOHN LANE
AT THE BODLEY HEAD
CHICAGO: A. C. McCLURG
AND CO.   1895

CONTENTS

CONTENTS

CONTENTS

Some of these Poems have appeared in THE PALL MALL GAZETTE, *and elsewhere*

AMBERGRIS

A

THE SPIDER QUEEN

In the deep heart of furthest fairyland
  Where foot of man has never trodden yet
The enchanted portals of her palace stand,
  And there her sleepless sentinels are set.

All round grow forests of white eglantine
  And drooping, dreaming clematis ; there blows
The purple nightshade ; there pale bindweeds twine
    And there the pale, frail flower of slumber
    grows.

Her palaces are decked with gleaming wings,
    Hung o'er with webs through spacious bower
    and hall,
Filled through and through with precious price-
    less things ;
    She is their mistress and she hates them all.

No darkling webs, woven in dust and gloom,
  Adorn her palace walls ; there gleam astir
Live threads of light, spun for a fairy's loom,
  And stolen by her slaves and brought to her.

She wears a robe woven of the July sun,
  Mixed with green threads won from the East
    at dawn,
Bordered with silver moonrays, finely spun,
  And gemmed with glowworms from some
    shadowy lawn.

She wears a crown of dewdrops bright like tears,
  Her girdle is a web of rainbow dyes ;
She knows no youth, nor age; the hours and
    years
  Leave never a shadow on her lips and eyes.

In magic rings of green and glistening light
  Her fairies dance, in star-spun raiment clad,
Her people do her bidding day and night,
  Her dark-robed servants toil to make her glad.

Her minstrels play to her—her singers raise
  Soft songs, more sweet than man has ever
    heard,

With endless rhythms of love her courtiers praise,
And all their heart is in their every word.

She is the mistress of all things that set
    Snare of fine webs to win their hearts' desire,
Queen of all folk who weave the death-strong net
    Between the poppy and the wild-rose briar.

Yet sits despair upon that brow of hers,
    And sorrow in her eyes makes festival ;
The soul of grief with her sad soul confers,
    And she sits lonely in her crowded hall ;

Because she has woven a web of her bright hair—
    A tear-bright web, to catch one soul ; and he
Beheld her, in her beauty, set the snare,
    And seeing laughed, and laughing passed out
        free !

THE GOLDEN ROSE

A poor lost princess, weary and worn,
  Came over the down by the wind-washed moor,
And the king looked out on her grace forlorn,
  And he took her in at his palace door.

He made her queen, he gave her a crown,
  Bidding her rest and be glad and gay
In his golden town, with a golden gown,
  And a new gold lily every day.

But the crown is heavy, the gold gown gray,
  And the queen's pale breast is like autumn
    snows ;
For he brings a gold lily every day,
  But no king gathers the golden rose.

One came at last to the palace keep
  By worlds of water and leagues of land,
Gray were his garments, his eyes were deep,
  And he held the golden rose in his hand.

She left gold gown, gold town, gold crown,
  And followed him straight to a world apart,
And he left her asleep on the wind-washed down,
  With the golden rose on her quiet heart.

INSPIRATION

I WANDERED in the enchanted wood,
  And as I wandered there, I sang
A song I never understood,
  Though sweet the music rang.

I held a lily white and fair,
  Its perfume was a song divine,
A song like moonlight and clear air,
  No rose-hued cloud like mine.

Beneath pale moon and wind-winged skies
  My lips were dumb as one drew near,
Folded warm wings across my eyes
  And whispered in my ear.

He left a flame-flower in my hand,
  And bade me sing as heretofore
The song I could not understand ;
  But I can sing no more.

His secret seals my dumb lips fast,
  My lily withered 'neath his wing ;
But now I understand at last
  The song I used to sing.

FLOWER OF ALOE

How can I tell you how I love you, dear ?'
  There is no music now the world is old ;
  The songs have all been sung, the tales all told
Broken the vows are all this many a year.

Had we but met when all the world was new,
  When virgin blossoms decked untrodden fields,
  I had plucked all the buds that summer yields
And woven a garland, worthy even of you.

Or had I sung when rhymes were yet unwed,
  And crowned their marriage in the songs I made,
  I had laid them down before you unafraid,
Meet offering to your grace and goodlihead.

But all the dreams are dreamed, and no new heat
  Touches life's altars, all the scents are burnt,
  The truths all taught and all the lessons learnt,
And no new stars lead kings to kiss Love's feet.

For now in this grey world, of youth bereft,
   Love has no throne, no sceptre and no crown ;
   His groves are hushed, his altars are cast down,
And we who worship—we have nothing left.

And yet—your lips !   The God has built him there
   An altar which has known nor flower nor flame :
   There may we burn the incense to Love's name,
There the immortal virgin rose be fair.

So—since my lips have known but one desire,
   And all my flowers of life are vowed to you—
   For us, at least, the old world has something
      new :
For me the altar—and for you the fire !

THE LOST EMBASSY

THE lilies lean to the white, white rose,
The sweet limes send to the blossomed trees,
Soft kisses borne by the golden bees—
And all the world is alive, awake,
And glad to the heart for the summer's sake.

From her tower window the Princess leant,
Where the white light butterflies came and went ;
She dropped soft kisses by twos and threes :
" White butterflies mine, will you carry these
To my Prince in prison ? for they, who knows,
May break the spell that has held him close,
And wake him and win him to stand up free
And laugh—in the sun—with me ! "

White lilies, gold in the golden sun,
White Princess, gold in your golden gown—
Far off lies the sad, enchanted town !
Bright wings, light wings, white wings that tire,
Though they carry the flower of the heart's desire—
Will you trust to these, too white, too slight
To bring back the fruit of heart's delight ?

All round and about the spell-bound town
The ways are dusty, the woods are brown ;

THE GIFT OF THE GODS

"GIVE me thy dreams," she said, and I,
    With empty hands and very poor,
Watched my fair flowery visions die
    Upon the temple's marble floor.

"Give joy," she said. I let joy go;
    I saw with cold, unclouded eyes
The crimson of the sunset glow
    Across the disenchanted skies.

"Give me thy youth," she said. I gave,
    And, sudden-clouded, died the sun,
And on the green mound of a grave
    Fell the slow raindrops, one by one.

"Give love," she cried. I gave that too.
    "Give beauty." Beauty sighed and fled;
For what on earth should beauty do,
    When love, who was her life, was dead?

She took the balm of innocent tears
   To hiss upon her altar-coal ;
She took the hopes of all my years,
   And, at the last, she took my soul.

With heart made empty of delight,
   And hands that held no more fair things,
I questioned her—" What shall requite
   The savour of my offerings ? "

"The Gods," she said, " with generous hand
   Give guerdon for thy gifts of cost—
Wisdom is thine—to understand
   The worth of all that thou hast lost ! "

LAVENDER

LULLABY

Sleep, sleep, my treasure,
The long day's pleasure
Has tired the birds, to their nests they creep ;
The garden still is
Alight with lilies,
But all the daisies are fast asleep.

Sleep, sleep, my darling,
Dawn wakes the starling,
The sparrow stirs when he sees day break ;
But all the meadow
Is wrapped in shadow,
And you must sleep till the daisies wake !

B

CHILD'S SONG IN SPRING

THE silver birch is a dainty lady,
    She wears a satin gown ;
The elm tree makes the old churchyard shady,
    She will not live in town.

The English oak is a sturdy fellow,
    He gets his green coat late ;
The willow is smart in a suit of yellow,
    While brown the beech trees wait.

Such a gay green gown God gives the larches—
    As green as He is good !
The hazels hold up their arms for arches
    When Spring rides through the wood.

The chestnut's proud, and the lilac's pretty,
    The poplar's gentle and tall,
But the plane tree's kind to the poor dull city—
    I love him best of all !

DREAM-DEW

WHITE bird of love, lie warm upon my breast,
  White flower of love, lie cool against my face !
  Teach me to dream again a little space
Ere this dream, too, sink earthward with the rest.

Teach me to dream my heart still pure as snow,
  Teach me to dream my lips deserve this grace :
  Then let me wake in some forgotten place,
And know you gone, but never see you go.

DAY AND NIGHT

NIGHT, ambushed in the darkling wood,
  Waited to seize the sleeping field,
His sentinels the pine trees stood
  Till the sun fell beneath his shield.
Then when the day at last was dead,
  Night, in his might, marched conquering,
Across the land his banner spread,
  And reigned as victor and as King.

And you and I—all days apart
  Rejoiced to see Night's victory,
Because he has a kindlier heart
  Than Day wears with his sovereignty :
Day keeps us prisoned close, but Night
  Lifts off Day's chains, and all night through
You dream of me, my life's delight,
  And all night through I dream of you.

THE SPELL

OUR boat has drifted with the stream
  That stirs the river's full sweet bosom,
And now she stays where gold flags gleam
  By meadow-sweet's pale foam of blossom.

Sedge-warblers sing the sun the song
  The nightingale sings to the shadows ;
Forget-me-nots grow all along
  The fringes of the happy meadows.

See the wet lilies' golden beads !
  The river-nymphs for necklace string them,
And in the sighing of the reeds
  You hear the song their lovers sing them.

Gold sun, blue air, green shimmering leaves,
  The weir's old song—the wood's old story—
Such spells the enchanting Summer weaves
  She holds me in a web of glory.

And you—with head against my arm
　And subtle wiles that seek to hold me—
Not even you can add a charm
　To the sweet sorceries that enfold me.

Yet lean there still!　The hour is ours;
　If we should move the charm might shiver
And joyless sun and scentless flowers
　Might mock a disenchanted river.

SEED-TIME AND HARVEST

My hollyhocks are all awake,
  And not a single rose is lost ;
My wallflowers, for dear pity's sake,
  Have fought the winter's cruel frost ;
Pink peony buds begin to peer,
  And flags push up their sword-blades fine :
I know there will not be this year
  A brighter garden plot than mine.

I'll sow the seeds of mignonette,
  Of snapdragon and sunflowers tall,
And scarlet poppies I will set
  To flower against the southern wall ;
Already all my lilies show
  The green crowns baby lilies wear,
And all my flowers will grow and blow,
  Because Love's hand has set them there.

I'll plant and water, sow and weed,
  Till not an inch of earth shows brown,
And take a vow of each small seed
  To grow to greenness and renown :
And then some day you'll pass my way,
  See gold and crimson, bell and star,
And catch my garden's soul, and say :
  " How sweet these cottage gardens are ! "

SURRENDER

THE wild wind wails in the poplar tree,
          I sit here alone.
O heart of my heart, come hither to me !
Come to me straight over land and sea,
          My soul—my own !

Not now—the clock's slow tick I hear,
          And nothing more.
The year is dying, the leaves are sere,
No ghost of the beautiful young crowned year
          Knocks at my door.

But one of these nights, a wild, late night,
          I, waiting within,
Shall hear your hand on the latch—and spite
Of prudence and folly and wrong and right,
          I shall let you in.

ROSE

SONG OF THE ROSE

THE lilac-time is over,
  Laburnum's day is past,
The red may-blossoms cover
  The white ones, fallen too fast.
And guelder-roses hang like snow,
Where purple flag-flowers grow.

And still the tulip lingers,
  The wall-flower's red like blood,
The ivy spreads pale fingers,
  The rose is in the bud.
Good-bye, sweet lilac, and sweet may !
The Rose is on the way.

You were but heralds sent us—
  All April's buds, and May's—
But painted missals lent us
  That we might learn her praise,
Might cast down every bud that blows
Before our Queen, the Rose !

MORNING

Dawn in the east, and chill dew falling—
    Tears of the new-born day ;
Dew on the lawn, and blackbirds calling,
    Music and mild mid-May.
The lilac, see, wins back the colour
    Lost on the field of Night ;
See, the spent stars grow dimmer, duller !
    Look forth, my life's delight !

Open your window, lean above me,
    Rose, my white rose, my song !
Leave your white nest, love, if you love me—
    Night is so lonely-long.
Day is our own, and day's a-breaking ;
    Sweet sleepy eyes of grey,
You shall not chide an early waking
    When Night grows kind as Day !

A GARDEN OF GIRLS

KATE is like a violet, Gertrude's like a rose,
  Jane is like a gillyflower smart ;
But Laura's like a lily, the purest bud that blows,
  Whose white, white petals veil the golden
    heart.
Girls in the garden—one and two and three—
One for song and one for play and one—ah, one for
    me !
Gillyflowers and violets and roses fair and fine,
But only one a lily, and that one lily mine !

Bertha is a hollyhock, stately, tall, and fair,
  Mabel has the daisy's dainty grace,
Edith has the gold of the sunflower on her hair,
  But Laura wears the lily in her face.
Girls in the garden—five and six and seven—
Three to take, and three to give, but one—ah ! one
    is given—
Hollyhocks and daisies, and sunflowers like the
    sun,
But only one a lily, and that one lily won.

MARGARET

I KNOW a garden where white lilies grow,
  Under the grey sweet-laden apple boughs ;
It is a garden where the roses blow,
  And honeysuckle covers half the house.
  O happy garden, do you keep the vows
Breathed in your quiet ear beneath the rose,
Or do you tell the tale to each soft wind that
    blows ?

Across your grassy paths she used to stray,
  She moved among you like a living flower,
Her beauty drank your beauty every day,
  Your beauty decked her beauty every hour.
  You gave her rose and lily for a dower,
With all sweet flowers and fruits your bosom
    bore—
She took them all—and now she comes not any
    more.

O garden, if you breathe such secret things
  To the south wind who loves you, tell him this :
To spread the scented softness of his wings,
  And seek that other garden where she is,
  And bid him bear no blossom and no kiss ;
Only, dear garden, tell the wind to say
How grey the world is grown since Margaret went
    away !

THE GLOW-WORM TO HER LOVE

BENEATH cool ferns, in dewy grass,
　Among the leaves that fringe the stream,
I hear the feet of lovers pass,
　—I hide all day, and dream.

But when the night, with wide soft wings,
　Droops on the trembling waiting wood,
And lulls the restless woodland things
　Within its solitude,

Ah, then my soft green lamp I light,
　That thou may'st find me by its fire—
Come, crown me, O my winged delight,
　My darling, my desire.

Yet they who praise the lamp I bear
　Have never a word of praise for thee,
My love, my life, my King of Air,
　Who lightest the lamp in me.

Thine, thine should be the praise they give
  My King, who art all praise above,
Since but for thee I dream and live,
  And light the lamp of love.

IN SANCTUARY

THE young Spring air was strong like wine,
 The sky reflected in your eyes
Was of a blue as deep-divine
 As ever glowed in southern skies.

We passed from out the sunny lane
 Into the green wood's shadowing ;
And, sudden, all Love's words seemed vain
 In that calm temple of the Spring.

Our god hears fair and tuneful words,
 And splendid flowers his altars bear ;
With choric song of leaves and birds,
 Another god was worshipped there.

Silent, we passed the woodland, through
 The coloured maze that Springtime weaves—
The light leaves dancing to the blue,
 The sunlight dancing to the leaves ;

I could not speak. I touched your hand
  At the green arch that ends the wood :
" Ah—if she should not understand ! "
  Ah—if you had not understood !

IN THE ROSE GARDEN

Red roses bright, pink roses and white
  That bud and blossom and fall ;
The very sight of my heart's delight
  Is more than worth them all !
Is worth far more than the whole sweet store
  That ever a garden grew—
She plucked the best to die at her breast,
  But it laughed and it bloomed anew !

The red rose lay at her lips to-day,
  And flushed with the joy thereof ;
She said a word that the white rose heard,
  And the white rose paled with love.
But the west wind blows, and my lady goes,
  And she leaves the world forlorn ;
And every rose that the garden grows,
  Might just as well be a thorn !

ROSEMARY

A SONG OF PARTINGS

DEDICATION

QUEEN of my Life, who gave me for my song
  The richest crown a poet ever wore,
Since I have given you songs a whole year long,
  Stoop, of your grace, and take this one song
  more.

I

It was upon a golden first June day
I chanced to take the quiet meadow way,
The flowers and grasses met across my feet—
Red sorrel, daisies, and pale meadow-sweet,
With buttercup that set the field ablaze—
The fields have no such flowers now-a-days—
The hedges all along were pearly white ;
And there I met with Chloris, all alone,
I drew her face to lean against my own.
The branch of May that hid her maiden eyes

Was scented like the rose of Paradise—
The May-bough fell : I knew what youth was
    worth,
And sunshine and the pleasant green-gowned earth,
When first love rhymed to summer and delight.
Yet, since my ship must sail away that day,
Despair new-born met new-born joy half-way.
And I, 'mid rapture and tears, found voice to say,
" Farewell—my Love—to leave you is to die,
I never shall forget you, dear !—Good-bye ! "

II

At parting from Clarinda life was gray,
With the cold haze of mutual weariness ;
The treasure our souls were bartered to possess,
We saw as ashes in the cold new day,
And only longed for leave to steal away
And wash remembrance from our tired eyes,
To cleanse our lips of kisses and of lies,
And to forget the barren fairy gold
For which we had journeyed such a weary road,
Had borne so hard a chain, so great a load,
Yet none the less was the old story told ;
The old refrain re-iterate none the less,
" My life's one love," we said, with sigh for sigh,
"I never can forget you, dear !—Good-bye ! "

III

You were so innocent, so sure, so shy,
Life was a chart well-marked for you, you knew—
With rocks and quicksands plainly set in view,
And, fitly beaconed by a heavenly star,
The port you sought marked unmistakeably,
Attainable, and not so very far.
So of your charity you chose to try
To take a pirate bark to haven with you.
Ah ! child, I had learned to steer on other seas,
Through other shoals—by other stars than these.
My chart had other ports you knew not of,
And so, one day, my black sails took the breeze,
And, ere you knew it, I was leagues away :
Yet not so far but you could hear me cry
Across the waters of your sheltered bay—
"Farewell, my child !   Farewell, my only love !
I never can forget you, dear !—Good-bye !"

IV

When I had courted Chloe half a year
She bade me go—she could not hold me dear,
We parted in the orchard, very late :
The dew lay on the white sweet clover flowers,

The moon shone through the pear-tree by the gate,
And on the grass the blossoms fell in showers.
" Pray Heaven," I cried, "to bless you—none the
    less
That you have cursed my life eternally ! "
She laughed—my pretty china shepherdess,
Kissed her white hand towards the white full moon.
" Up there," she said, "the folk who say farewell
Never intone it to a funeral bell,
But sing it to the sweet old-fashioned tune !
Go there and learn ! "—" I have learned that tune,"
    quoth I,
" 'I never can forget you, dear !—Good-bye !' "

V

In that far land where myrtles dream of love,
Where soft winds whisper through the orange
    grove ;
And, 'twixt the sapphire of the seas and skies,
The sunshine of perpetual summer lies,
I brought white flowers to lie where Clemence lay.
The shutters, closed, strove with the radiant day,
And in her villa all was still and chill.
Flowers die, they say, but these flowers never will,—
Whenever I see a rose I smell them still ;

I laid them by her on the strait white bed :
There were no kisses given, no tears were shed,
And never a whisper of farewell was said ;
Yet, when they had laid her underneath the clay,
And paid their prayers and tears, and gone their
    way,
My heart stirred, and I found the old word to say—
This time—this one time—and this last time—
    true :
" White lady, my white flowers touch you where
    you lie,
I never shall forget you !   Dear, good-bye ! "

Envoy.

Queen of my life, and of the songs I sing,
Whose love sets life to such a royal tune ;
This song of parting to your hands I bring,
As I bring honour and faith and everything :
Because I know our parting shall be soon—
Since violets hardly live one happy moon,
And love, full-fledged, is ready to take wing ;
But, when he flies, part we the silent way,
And, if you ever loved me, do not say :
" Farewell, my only love—I love you still,
I never will forget you ! "—For you will !

THE GHOST

Now that the curtains are drawn close,
    Now that the fire burns low,
And on her narrow bed the rose
    Is stark laid out in snow ;
Now that the wind of winter blows
Bid my heart say if still it knows
    The step it used to know.

I hear the silken gown you wear
    Sweep on the gallery floor,
Your step comes up the wide, dark stair
    And pauses at my door.
My heart with the old hope flowers fair—
That shrivels to the old despair,
    For you come in no more !

THE WAY OF THE WOOD

WHERE baby oaks play in the breeze
  Among wood-sorrel and fringed fern,
Through the green garments of the trees
  The quivering shafts of sunlight burn,

And all along the wet green ride,
  The dripping hazel-boughs between,
The spotted orchis, stiff with pride,
  Stands guard before the eglantine.

Sweet chestnuts droop their long, sharp leaves
  By knotted tree roots, mossed and brown,
Round which the honeysuckle weaves
  Its scented golden wild-wood crown.

O wood, last year you saw us meet,
  For her your leaves and buds were gay,
Your moss spread velvet for her feet.
  Your flowers upon her bosom lay.

This year you wear your raiment bright,
  As fair as ever yet you wore.
And, none the less, the world's delight
  Walks in your ways no more, no more.

QUIETA NE MOVETE

DEAR, if I told you, made your sorrow certain,
  Showed you the ghosts that o'er my pillow lean,
What joy were mine—to cast aside the curtain
  And clasp you close with no base lies between !

You have given all, and still would find to give
      me
  More love, more tenderness than ever yet :
You would forgive me—ah, you would forgive me,
  But all your life you never would forget.

And I, thank God, can still in your embraces
  Forget the past, with all its strife and stain,
—But if you, too, beheld the evil faces,
  I should forget them never, never again !

ENVOYS

Brown leaves forget the green of May,
 The earth forgets the kiss of Spring ;
And down our happy woodland way
 Gray mists go wandering.

You have forgotten too, they say ;
 Yet, does no stealthy memory creep
Among the mist wreaths, ghostly gray,
 Where spell-bound violets sleep ?

Ah, send your thought sometimes to stray
 By paths that knew our lingering feet.
My thought walks there this many a day,
 And they, at least, may meet.

D

THE GARDEN

CHOKED with ill weeds my garden lay a-dying,
  Hard was the ground, no bud had heart to blow,
Yet shone your smile there, with your soft breath
    sighing :
  "Have patience, for some day the flowers will
    grow."

Some weeds you killed, you made a plot and tilled
    it ;
  "My plot," you said, "rich harvest yet shall
    give,"
With sun-warmed seeds of hope your dear hands
    filled it,
  With rain-soft tears of pity bade them live.

So, weak among the weeds that had withstood
    you,
  One little pure white flower grew by-and-by ;
You could not pluck my flower—alas ! how should
    you ?
  You sowed the seed, but let the blossom die.

THROUGH THE WOOD

THROUGH the wood, the green wood, the wet wood,
    the light wood,
  Love and I went maying a thousand lives ago ;
Shafts of golden sunlight had made a golden bright
    wood
    In my heart reflected, because I loved you so.

Through the wood, the chill wood, the brown wood,
    the bare wood,
  I alone went lonely no later than last year,
What had thinned the branches, and wrecked my
    dear and fair wood,
    Killed the pale wild roses and left the rose-
    thorns sere ?

Through the wood, the dead wood, the sad wood,
    the lone wood,
  Winds of winter shiver through lichens old and
    grey,
You ride past forgetting the wood that was our
    own wood,   .
    All our own—and withered as ever a flower of
    May.

A KENTISH GARDEN

THERE is a grey-walled garden, far away
   From noise and smoke of cities, where the hours
   Pass with soft wings among the happy flowers,
And lovely leisure blossoms every day.

There, tall and white, the sceptral lily blows ;
   There grow the pansy, pink, and columbine,
   Brave hollyhocks, and star-white jessamine,
And the red glory of the royal rose.

There greeny glow-worms gem the dusky lawn,
   The lime-trees breathe their fragrance to the
       night,
   Pink roses sleep, and dream that they are
       white,
Until they wake to colour with the dawn.

There, in the splendour of the sultry noon,
   The sunshine sleeps upon the garden bed
   Where the white poppy droops a drowsy head
And dreams of kisses from the white full moon.

And there, some days, all wild with wind and
    rain,
  The tossed trees show the white side of their
    leaves,
  While the great drops drip from the ivied
    eaves,
And birds are still—till the sun shines again.

And there, all days, my heart goes wandering,
  Because there, first, my heart began to know
  The glories of the summer and the snow,
The loveliness of harvest and of spring.

There may be fairer gardens ; but I know
  There is no other garden half so dear ;
  Because 'tis there, this many, many a year,
The sacred, sweet, white flowers of memory grow !

MYRRH

THE PAST

MAKE strong your door with bolt and bar,
  Make every window fast ;
Strong brass and iron as they are,
  They are so easy passed—
So easy broken and cast aside,
  And by the open door
My footsteps come to your guarded home,
  And pass away no more.

In the golden noon—by the lovers' moon,
  My shadow bars your way,
My shroud shows white in the blackest night
  And grey in the gladdest day.
And by your board and by your bed
  There is a place for me,
And in the glow when the coals burn low,
  My face is the face ye see.

I come between when ye laugh and lean,
   I burn in the tears ye weep:
I am there when ye wake in the gray day-break
   From the gold of a lovers' sleep.
I wither the rose and I spoil the song,
   And Death is not strong to save—
For I shall creep while your mourners weep,
   And wait for you in your grave.

THE BETTER PART

THERE's a grey old church on a wind-swept hill
  Where three bent yew trees cower,
The gipsy roses grow there still,
  And the thyme and Saint John's gold flower,
The pale blue violets that love the chalk
  Cling light round the lichened stone,
And starlings chatter and grey owls talk
  In the belfry o' nights alone.

It's a thousand leagues and a thousand years
  From the brick-built, gas-lit town
To the little church where the wild thyme hears
  The bees and the breeze of the down.
The town is crowded and hard and rough ;
  Let those fight in its press who will—
But the little churchyard is quiet enough,
  And there's room in the churchyard still.

THE GRAY FOLK

The house, with blind unhappy face,
  Stands lonely in the last year's corn,
  And in the grayness of the morn
The gray folk come about the place.

By many pathways, gliding gray
  They come past meadow, wood, and wold,
  Come by the farm and by the fold
From the green fields of yesterday.

Past lock and chain and bolt and bar
  They press, to stand about my bed,
  And like the faces of the dead
I know their hidden faces are.

They will not leave me in the day
  And when night falls they will not go,
  Because I silenced, long ago,
The only voice that they obey.

THE TREASURE

UNDER our lead we lie
While the sun and the snow go by,
    And our shrouds lie close, lie close,
    Like the leaves of a shut white rose
    That knows not what summer knows
Before it is time to die.

You, in the sun, up there
Where the wild thyme scents the air ;
    Is it warm still—and sweet and gay
    Up there in the wide blue day ?
    Do you pity us, shut away
From the fields where the flowers are fair ?

Pity us here ? shut in
In the dark, where the flowers begin ?
    The coins lie light on our eyes,
    In our empty hands is the prize,
    The treasure that fools and wise
Are breaking their hearts to win !

NEW YEAR SNOW

THE white snow falls on hill and dale,
  The snow falls white by square and street,
Falls on the town, a bridal veil,
  And on the fields a winding-sheet.

A winding-sheet for last year's flowers,
  For last year's love, and last year's tear,
A bridal veil for the New Hours,
  For the New Love and the New Year.

Soft snow, spread out his winding-sheet !
  Spin fine her veil, O bridal snow !
Cover the print of her dancing feet,
  And the place where he lies low.

LOVE'S GUERDONS

DEAREST, if I almost cease to weep for you,
  Do not doubt I love you just the same ;
'Tis because my life has grown to keep for you
  All the hours that sorrow does not claim.

All the hours when I may steal away to you,
  Where you lie alone through the long day,
Lean my face against your turf and say to you
  All that there is no one else to say.

Do they let you listen—do you lean to me ?
  Know now what in life you never knew,
When I whisper all that you have been to me,
  All that I might never be to you ?

Dear, lie still. No tears but mine are shed for you,
  No one else leaves kisses day by day,
No one's heart but mine has beat and bled for you,
  No one else's flowers push mine away.

No one else remembers—do not call to her,
  Not alone she treads the churchyard grass ;
You are nothing now who once were all to her,
  Do not call her—let the strangers pass !

MUSK

INDISCRETION

RED tulip-buds last night caressed
The sacred ivory of her breast.
She met me, eager to divine
What gold-heart bud of hope was mine.

Nor eyes nor lips were strong to part
The close-curled petals round my heart ;
The joy I knew no monarch knows,
Yet not a petal would unclose.

But, ah !—the tulip-buds, unwise,
Warmed with the sunshine of her eyes,
And by her soft breath glorified,
Went mad with love and opened wide.

She saw their hearts, all golden-gay,
Laughed, frowned, and flung the flowers away.
Poor flowers, in Heaven as you were,
Why did you show your hearts to her ?

THE INVITATION

DELIA, my dear, delightful Lady,
  Time flies in town, you say,
  New gowns shine fresh as May,
  The Park is glad and gay,
Ah—but the woods are green and shady—
  Come, Delia, come away!

The crown your kneeling slaves award you
  Is beauty's royal right;
  Your beauty, Delia, might
  Win crowns more sweet, more bright:
Your niggard world will not afford you
  The crown of Heart's delight.

Sable your court will wear—to lose you;
  My garden's dressed in green,
  Such buds its leaves between
  As never yet were seen;
There is no flower it can refuse you—
  Come to your King, my Queen!

MUSK

TO ONE WHO BADE HIM WORK

EACH day Work bids my heart anew,
  Fold wings and watch my brain at play ;
  But brain and heart will fly your way,
And find their natural home in you !
  Come to me—'tis the only way !

For heart and brain have had to learn
  Such carrier-pigeon feats of flight,
  That were you here, my heart's delight,
My brain and heart to Work would turn,
  Spread wings, and flutter from your sight.

THE CLAIM

Oh! I admit I'm dull and poor,
  And plain and gloomy, as you tell me;
And dozens flock around your door
  Who in all points but one excel me.

You smile on them, on me you frown,
  They worship for the wage you pay;
I lay life, love, and honour down
  For you to walk on every day.

I am the only one who sees
  That though such gifts can never move
    you,
A meagre price are gifts like these
  For life's high privilege—to love you.

I am the one among your train
  Who sees that loving you is worth
A thousand times the certain gain
  Of all the heaped-up joys of earth.

And you, who know as well as I,
  What your glass tells you every morning—
A kindred soul you should descry,
  Dilute with sympathy your scorning.

At least you should approve the intense
  Love that gives all for you to waste ;
Your other lovers have more sense,
  Admit that I have better taste.

TO HIS LADY

(Who asked a Song in Spring)

WHY do you bid your poet sing,
  Who has no mind to song—
Who only wants to see the Spring,
  Long sought and tarrying long ?
The shivering, dreary winter through
  My song enshrined my vow ;
If then my songs were sweet to you,
  Let me be silent now !

Have I not duly sung, my dear,
  Your goodness and your grace ?
Now that your rival, Spring, is here,
  O let me see her face !
The hedge is white with buds of May,
  The fields are green with Spring,
Oh, give your bard a holiday :
  He does not want to sing !

He wants to listen ; all alone,
  He wants to steal away
To hear the ring-doves' tender tone,
  And what the thrushes say.
He wants to hear what can't be heard
  When you and love are near—
The sweet Spring's soft and secret word ;
  Oh, let him go, my dear !

THE CHARM

LIKE crimson lamps the tulips swing,
The lily flowers their incense bring,
The daisies votive garlands fling
Before the altar of the Spring.

And you and I in this green May,
When thrushes sing, and white lambs play,
Go glad at heart—so glad and gay,
No word seems good enough to say.

Yet there's a charm, it would appear,
Which, if I spoke it in your ear,
Would fix the spring for ever here ;
Pass on—I will not speak it, dear.

DEFERRED

NOT now, when skies are gold and blue
And you have me and I have you,
When there are roses all the way,
And April days and nights of May,
And life is joy the whole day long—
Not now can passion flower in song.

But in the dark days by-and-by,
When, deep divided, you and I,
Shivering among the rose-thorns bare,
At last confess what fools we were ;
Then, neatly wired, a nosegay fine
Shall deck your heart—O heart of mine !

SPRING SONG

ALL winter through I sat alone,
  Doors barred and windows shuttered fast,
And listened to the wind's faint moan,
  And ghostly mutterings of the past ;
And in the pauses of the rain,
  'Mid whispers of dead sorrow and sin,
Love tapped upon the window pane :
  I had no heart to let him in.

But now, with spring, my doors stand wide ;
  My windows let delight creep through ;
I hear the skylark sing outside ;
  I see the crocus, golden new.
The pigeons on my window-sill,
  Winging and wooing, flirt and flout,—
Now Love must enter if he will,
  I have no heart to keep him out.

BERGAMOT

VILLEGGIATURE

My window, framed in pear-tree bloom,
  White-curtained shone, and softly lighted :
So, by the pear-tree, to my room
  Your ghost last night climbed uninvited.

Your solid self, long leagues away,
  Deep in dull books, had hardly missed me ;
And yet you found this Romeo's way,
  And through the blossom climbed and kissed
    me.

I watched the still and dewy lawn,
  The pear-tree boughs hung white above you ;
I listened to you till the dawn,
  And half forgot I did not love you.

Oh, dear ! what pretty things you said,
  What pearls of song you threaded for me !
I did not—till your ghost had fled—
  Remember how you always bore me !

TOWN AND COUNTRY

The Sun tells to Trafalgar Square
   His old and radiant story,
And touches in the young spring air
   The pepper-pots to glory.

Spring's robe down Piccadilly floats,
   The parks glow with her treasure,
And button-holes of morning coats
   Rhyme with her royal pleasure.

Now persons beautifully dressed
   In Bond-street shop and saunter,
And town—by Spring's soft breath caressed—
   Would as its mistress vaunt her.

But far away from square and street,
   Where willows shine and shiver,
The splendour of her silver feet
   Is on the wood and river.

She laughs among the tree-roots brown,
   Among the dewy clover,
For Spring coquets but with the town ;
   The country is her lover.

REJECTED

WE wandered down the meadow way—
  The path beside the hedge is shady,—
You did not see the silver may,
  You talked of Art, my sweet blind Lady.

You talked of values and of tone,
  Of square touch and New English crazes ;
Could you not see we were alone,
  Where God's hand paints the world with
    daisies ?

You spoke of Paris and of Rome
  And in the hedgerow's thorny shadows
A white-throat sang a song of home,
  Of English lanes and English meadows.

You talked about the aims of Art
  And how all Art must needs be moral ;
I heard you with a sinking heart
  And watched the waving crimson sorrel.

For when I found you had not heard
  The song—nor seen the dewy clover,
I cared no more to find the word
  Should make you hear and see a lover !

F

COMPENSATION

LADY, I see you every day—
  More than your other lovers do ;
I sit beside you at the Play,
  And in the Park I ride with you.

Through picture shows with you I roam
  With you I shop and dance and dine ;
I know the hours when you're " at home '
  To no one else's knock but mine.

And yet so near and yet so far,
  I scarce dare look at you, for fear
I should remark, " How sweet you are,
  How charming, and how very dear ! "

I dare not touch that hand of yours,
  Or lend my voice a tender tone ;
I know my state of grace endures
  By fasting and by prayer alone.

But, in my lonely dreamlit nights,
  I kiss your hands, your lips, your eyes ;
For absence grants me all the rights
  Your presence evermore denies.

THE LAST DITCH

Love, through your varied views on Art
  Untiring have I followed you,
Content to know I had your heart
  And was your Art-ideal, too.

As, dear, I was when first we met.
  ('Twas at the time you worshipped Leighton,
And were attempting to forget
  Your Foster and your Noel Paton.)

"Love rhymes with Art," said your dear voice,
  And, at my crude, uncultured age,
I could but blushingly rejoice
  That you had passed the Rubens stage.

When Madox Brown and Morris swayed
  Your taste, did I not dress and look
Like any Middle Ages maid
  In an illuminated book ?

I wore strange garments, without shame,
  Of formless form and toneless tones,
I might have stepped out of the frame
  Of a Rossetti or Burne-Jones.

I stole soft frills from Marcus Stone,
  My waist wore Herkomer's disguise,
My slender purse was strained, I own,
  But—my silk lay as Sargent's lies.

And when you were abroad—in Prague—
  'Mid Cherets I had shone, a star ;
Then for your sake I grew as vague
  As Mr Whistler's ladies are.

But now at last you sue in vain,
  For here a life's submission ends :
Not even for you will I grow plain
  As Aubrey Beardsley's "lady friends."

Here I renounce your hand—unless
  You find your Art-ideal elsewhere ;
I *will not* wear the kind of dress
  That Laurence Housman's people wear!

THE CHOICE

PLAGUE take the dull and dusty town,
  Its paved and sordid mazes,
Now Spring has trimmed her pretty gown
  With buttercups and daisies !

With half my heart I long to lie
  Among the flowered grasses,
And hear the loving leaves that sigh
  As their sweet Mistress passes.

Through picture-shows I make my way
  While flower-crowned maids go maying,
And all the cultured things I say
  That cultured folk are saying.

For I renounce Spring's darling face,
  With may-bloom fresh upon it :
My Mistress lives in Grosvenor-place
  And wears a Bond-street bonnet !

A COMEDY

Madam, you bade me act a part,
  A comedy of your devising—
Forbade me to consult my heart,
  To be sincere—or compromising.

The play was not my own device,
  My stage-struck youth lies far behind me ;
And yet—I thought it would be nice
  To play the part that you assigned me.

Thus have I learned my rôle so well
  That, as I play, you question whether
Fate has not taught your jest a spell
  To bind me to you altogether.

The truth is this : so ill I wrought
  In mastering the part you gave me,
That now 'tis tyrant of my thought,
  And nothing in the world can save me !

Between me and my work, your face,
  In haunting fashion, daily lingers ;
Your eyes make mine their dwelling place
  Your dream-hand thrills my idle fingers.

Through death-white nights I dream of you—
  Of what might move, and what has moved
    you—
Ah ! no ! There's nothing you can do ! . . .
  . . . It's not as though I really loved you.

THE END

ADIEU, Madame! The moon of May
Wanes now above the orchard grey;
The white May-blossoms fall like snow,
As Love foretold a month ago—
Or was it only yesterday?

All pleasant things must pass away;
You would not, surely, have me stay?
I own I shun the inference! No!
      Adieu, Madame!

Come, dry your eyes, for not this way
Should end your pretty pastoral play.
You have no heart—you told me so—
And I adore you, as you know;
Smile, while I break my heart and say
      Adieu, Madame!

TURNBULL AND SPEARS, PRINTERS, EDINBURGH.

JOHN LANE

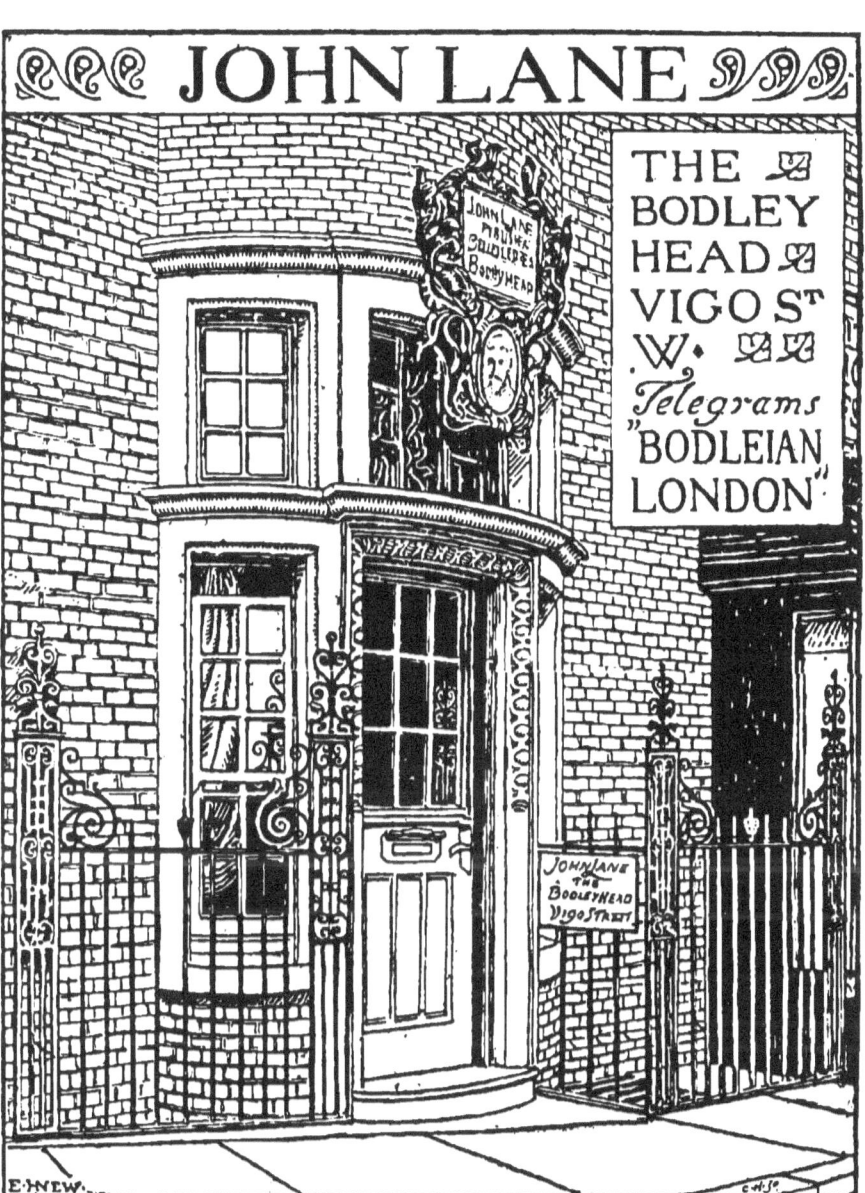

THE BODLEY HEAD VIGO ST W.
Telegrams "BODLEIAN LONDON"

E. NEW.

CATALOGUE of PUBLICATIONS in BELLES LETTRES all at net prices

List of Books

IN

BELLES LETTRES

(Including some Transfers)

Published by John Lane

The Bodley Head

VIGO STREET, LONDON, W.

N.B.—The Authors and Publisher reserve the right of reprinting any book in this list if a new edition is called for, except in cases where a stipulation has been made to the contrary, and of printing a separate edition of any of the books for America irrespective of the numbers to which the English editions are limited. The numbers mentioned do not include copies sent to the public libraries, nor those sent for review.

Most of the books are published simultaneously in England and America, and in many instances the names of the American Publishers are appended.

———◆———

ADAMS (FRANCIS).
    ESSAYS IN MODERNITY. Crown 8vo. 5s. net. [*Shortly.*
        Chicago : Stone & Kimball.
    A CHILD OF THE AGE. (*See* KEYNOTES SERIES.)

ALLEN (GRANT).
    THE LOWER SLOPES: A Volume of Verse. With Title-page and Cover Design by J. ILLINGWORTH KAY. 600 copies. Crown 8vo. 5s. net.
        Chicago : Stone & Kimball.
    THE WOMAN WHO DID. (*See* KEYNOTES SERIES.)
    THE BRITISH BARBARIANS. (*See* KEYNOTES SERIES.)

BAILEY (JOHN C).
    AN ANTHOLOGY OF ENGLISH ELEGIES. [*In preparation.*

BEARDSLEY (AUBREY).
THE STORY OF VENUS AND TANNHÄUSER, in which is set forth an exact account of the Manner of State held by Madam Venus, Goddess and Meretrix, under the famous Hörselberg, and containing the adventures of Tannhäuser in that place, his repentance, his journeying to Rome, and return to the loving mountain. By AUBREY BEARDSLEY. With 20 full-page Illustrations, numerous ornaments, and a cover from the same hand. Sq. 16mo. 10s. 6d. net. [*In preparation.*

BEDDOES (T. L.).
See GOSSE (EDMUND).

BEECHING (REV. H. C.).
IN A GARDEN: Poems. With Title-page designed by ROGER FRY. Crown 8vo. 5s. net.
New York: Macmillan & Co.

BENSON (ARTHUR CHRISTOPHER).
LYRICS. Fcap. 8vo, buckram. 5s. net.
New York: Macmillan & Co.

BRIDGES (ROBERT).
SUPPRESSED CHAPTERS AND OTHER BOOKISHNESS. Crown 8vo. 3s. 6d. net.
New York: Charles Scribner's Sons.

BROTHERTON (MARY).
ROSEMARY FOR REMEMBRANCE. With Title-page and Cover Design by WALTER WEST. Fcap. 8vo. 3s. 6d. net.

BUCHAN (JOHN).
MUSA PISCATRIX. [*In preparation.*

CAMPBELL (GERALD).
THE JONESES AND THE ASTERISKS. (*See* MAYFAIR SET.)

CASE (ROBERT).
AN ANTHOLOGY OF ENGLISH EPITHALAMIES.
[*In preparation.*

CASTLE (MRS EGERTON).
MY LITTLE LADY ANNE. (*See* PIERROT'S LIBRARY.)

CASTLE (EGERTON).
See STEVENSON (ROBERT LOUIS).

CRAIG (R. MANIFOLD).
THE SACRIFICE OF FOOLS: A Novel. Crown 8vo. 4s. 6d. net. [*In preparation.*

CRANE (WALTER).

TOY BOOKS. Re-issue. Each with new Cover Design and
end papers. 9d. net.

The group of three bound in one volume, with a decorative cloth cover, end papers, and a newly written and
designed preface. 3s. 6d. net.

I. THIS LITTLE PIG.
II. THE FAIRY SHIP.
III. KING LUCKIEBOY'S PARTY.
Chicago : Stone & Kimball.

CROSSE (VICTORIA).

THE WOMAN WHO DIDN'T. (See KEYNOTES SERIES.)

DALMON (C. W.).

SONG FAVOURS. With a Title-page designed by J. P.
DONNE. Sq. 16mo. 3s. 6d. net.
Chicago : Way & Williams.

D'ARCY (ELLA).

MONOCHROMES. (See KEYNOTES SERIES.)

DAVIDSON (JOHN).

PLAYS : An Unhistorical Pastoral ; A Romantic Farce ;
Bruce, a Chronicle Play ; Smith, a Tragic Farce ;
Scaramouch in Naxos, a Pantomime, with a Frontis-
piece and Cover Design by AUBREY BEARDSLEY.
Printed at the Ballantyne Press. 500 copies. Small
4to. 7s. 6d. net.
Chicago : Stone & Kimball.

FLEET STREET ECLOGUES. Fcap. 8vo, buckram. 5s.
net.   [Out of Print at present.

A RANDOM ITINERARY AND A BALLAD. With a Frontispiece and Title-page by LAURENCE HOUSMAN.
600 copies. Fcap. 8vo, Irish Linen. 5s. net.
Boston : Copeland & Day.

BALLADS AND SONGS. With a Title-page and Cover
Design by WALTER WEST. Third Edition. Fcap.
8vo, buckram. 5s. net.
Boston : Copeland & Day.

DAWE (W. CARLTON).

YELLOW AND WHITE. (See KEYNOTES SERIES.)

DE TABLEY (LORD).
   POEMS, DRAMATIC AND LYRICAL. By JOHN LEICESTER
    WARREN (Lord De Tabley). Illustrations and Cover
    Design by C. S. RICKETTS. Second Edition. Crown
    8vo. 7s. 6d. net.
    New York : Macmillan & Co.
   POEMS, DRAMATIC AND LYRICAL. Second Series, uni-
    form in binding with the former volume. Crown 8vo.
    5s. net.
    New York : Macmillan & Co.

DIX (GERTRUDE).
   THE GIRL FROM THE FARM. (*See* KEYNOTES SERIES.)

DOSTOIEVSKY (F.).
   See KEYNOTES SERIES, Vol. III.

ECHEGARAY (JOSÉ).
   See LYNCH (HANNAH).

EGERTON (GEORGE).
   KEYNOTES. (*See* KEYNOTES SERIES.)
   DISCORDS. (*See* KEYNOTES SERIES.)
   YOUNG OFEG'S DITTIES. A translation from the Swedish
    of OLA HANSSON. With Title-page and Cover Design
    by AUBREY BEARDSLEY. Crown 8vo. 3s. 6d. net.
    Boston : Roberts Bros.

FARR (FLORENCE).
   THE DANCING FAUN. (*See* KEYNOTES SERIES.)

FLEMING (GEORGE).
   FOR PLAIN WOMEN ONLY. (*See* MAYFAIR SET.)

FLETCHER (J. S.).
   THE WONDERFUL WAPENTAKE. By 'A SON OF THE
    SOIL.' With 18 full-page Illustrations by J. A.
    SYMINGTON. Crown 8vo. 5s. 6d. net.
    Chicago : A. C. McClurg & Co.

FREDERIC (HAROLD).
   MRS ALBERT GRUNDY. (*See* MAYFAIR SET.)

GALE (NORMAN).
   ORCHARD SONGS. With Title-page and Cover Design
    by J. ILLINGWORTH KAY. Fcap 8vo, Irish Linen.
    5s. net.
    Also a Special Edition limited in number on hand-made paper
    bound in English vellum. £1, 1s. net.
    New York : G. P. Putnam's Sons.

GARNETT (RICHARD).
  POEMS. With Title-page by J. ILLINGWORTH KAY.
    350 copies. Crown 8vo. 5s. net.
      Boston : Copeland & Day.
  DANTE, PETRARCH, CAMOENS, cxxiv Sonnets rendered
    in English. Crown 8vo. 5s. net. [*In preparation.*

GEARY (NEVILL).
  A LAWYER'S WIFE : A Novel. Crown 8vo. 4s. 6d.
    net. [*In preparation.*

GOSSE (EDMUND).
  THE LETTERS OF THOMAS LOVELL BEDDOES. Now
    first edited. Pott 8vo. 5s. net.
    Also 25 copies large paper. 12s. 6d. net.
      New York : Macmillan & Co.

GRAHAME (KENNETH).
  PAGAN PAPERS : A Volume of Essays. With Title-
    page by AUBREY BEARDSLEY. Fcap. 8vo. 5s. net.
      Chicago : Stone & Kimball.
  THE GOLDEN AGE. Crown 8vo. 3s. 6d. net.
      Chicago : Stone & Kimball.

GREENE (G. A.).
  ITALIAN LYRISTS OF TO-DAY. Translations in the
    original metres from about thirty-five living Italian
    poets, with bibliographical and biographical notes.
    Crown 8vo. 5s. net.
      New York : Macmillan & Co.

GREENWOOD (FREDERICK).
  IMAGINATION IN DREAMS. Crown 8vo. 5s. net.
      New York : Macmillan & Co.

HAKE (T. GORDON).
  A SELECTION FROM HIS POEMS. Edited by Mrs
    MEYNELL. With a Portrait after D. G. ROSSETTI,
    and a Cover Design by GLEESON WHITE. Crown
    8vo. 5s. net.
      Chicago : Stone and Kimball.

HANSSON (LAURA MARHOLM).
  MODERN WOMEN : Six Psychological Sketches. [Sophia
    Kovalevsky, George Egerton, Eleanora Duse, Amalie
    Skram, Marie Bashkirtseff, A. Edgren Leffler.] Trans-
    lated from the German by HERMIONE RAMSDEN.
    Crown 8vo. 3s. 6d. net. [*In preparation.*

HANSSON (OLA). *See* EGERTON.

HARLAND (HENRY).
GREY ROSES. (*See* KEYNOTES SERIES.)

HAYES (ALFRED).
THE VALE OF ARDEN AND OTHER POEMS. With a
Title-page and a Cover designed by E. H. NEW.
Fcap. 8vo. 3s. 6d. net.
Also 25 copies large paper. 15s. net.

HEINEMANN (WILLIAM).
THE FIRST STEP. A Dramatic Moment. Small 4to.
3s. 6d. net.

HOPPER (NORA).
BALLADS IN PROSE. With a Title-page and Cover by
WALTER WEST. Sq. 16mo. 5s. net.
Boston : Roberts Bros.
A VOLUME OF POEMS. With Title-page designed by
PATTEN WILSON. Sq. 16mo. 5s. net.
[*In preparation.*

HOUSMAN (CLEMENCE).
THE WERE WOLF. With six Full-page Illustrations,
Title-page and Cover Design, by LAURENCE HOUS-
MAN. Sq. 16mo. 4s. net. [*In preparation.*

HOUSMAN (LAURENCE).
GREEN ARRAS : Poems. With Illustrations by the
Author. Crown 8vo. 5s. net. [*In preparation.*

IRVING (LAURENCE).
GODEFROI AND YOLANDE : A Play. With three Illus-
trations by AUBREY BEARDSLEY. Sm. 4to. 5s. net.
[*In preparation.*

JAMES (W. P.).
ROMANTIC PROFESSIONS : A Volume of Essays. With
Title - page designed by J. ILLINGWORTH KAY.
Crown 8vo. 5s. net.
New York : Macmillan & Co.

JOHNSON (LIONEL).
THE ART OF THOMAS HARDY : Six Essays. With Etched
Portrait by WM. STRANG, and Bibliography by JOHN
LANE. Second Edition. Crown 8vo. 5s. 6d. net.
Also 150 copies, large paper, with proofs of the portrait. £1, 1s.
net.
New York : Dodd, Mead & Co.

JOHNSON (PAULINE).
> WHITE WAMPUM : Poems.   With a Title-page and Cover
> Design by E. H. NEW.   Crown 8vo.   5s. net.
>> Boston : Lamson, Wolffe & Co.

JOHNSTONE (C. E.).
> BALLADS OF BOY AND BEAK.   With a Title-page designed
> by F. H. TOWNSEND.   Sq. 32mo.   2s. 6d. net.
>> *[In preparation.*

KEYNOTES SERIES.
> Each volume with specially designed Title-page by AUBREY
> BEARDSLEY.   Crown 8vo, cloth.   3s. 6d. net.

Vol.   I. KEYNOTES.   By GEORGE EGERTON.
[Seventh edition now ready.

Vol.   II. THE DANCING FAUN.   By FLORENCE FARR.

Vol.   III. POOR FOLK.   Translated from the Russian of
F. Dostoievsky by LENA MILMAN.   With a Preface
by GEORGE MOORE.

Vol.   IV. A CHILD OF THE AGE.   By FRANCIS ADAMS.

Vol.   V. THE GREAT GOD PAN AND THE INMOST
LIGHT.   By ARTHUR MACHEN.
[Second edition now ready.

Vol.   VI. DISCORDS.   By GEORGE EGERTON.
[Fourth edition now ready.

Vol.   VII. PRINCE ZALESKI.   By M. P. SHIEL.

Vol.   VIII. THE WOMAN WHO DID.   By GRANT ALLEN.
[Eighteenth edition now ready.

Vol.   IX. WOMEN'S TRAGEDIES.   By H. D. LOWRY.

Vol.   X. GREY ROSES.   By HENRY HARLAND.

Vol.   XI. AT THE FIRST CORNER AND OTHER STORIES.
By H. B. MARRIOTT WATSON.

Vol.   XII. MONOCHROMES.   By ELLA D'ARCY.

Vol.   XIII. AT THE RELTON ARMS.   By EVELYN SHARP.

Vol.   XIV. THE GIRL FROM THE FARM.   By GERTRUDE
DIX.

Vol.   XV. THE MIRROR OF MUSIC.   By STANLEY V.
MAKOWER.

Vol.   XVI. YELLOW AND WHITE.   By W. CARLTON
DAWE.

Vol. XVII. THE   MOUNTAIN   LOVERS.   By FIONA
MACLEOD.

Vol. XVIII. THE WOMAN WHO DIDN'T.   By VICTORIA
CROSSE.   *[Second edition now ready.*

KEYNOTES SERIES—*continued.*
The following are in rapid preparation.
Vol. XIX. THE THREE IMPOSTORS. By ARTHUR MACHEN.
Vol. XX. NOBODY'S FAULT. By NETTA SYRETT.
Vol. XXI. THE BRITISH BARBARIANS. By GRANT ALLEN.
Vol. XXII. IN HOMESPUN. By E. NESBIT.
Vol. XXIII. PLATONIC AFFECTIONS. By JOHN SMITH.
Vol. XXIV. NETS FOR THE WIND. By UNA TAYLOR.
Vol. XXV. ORANGE AND GREEN. By CALDWELL LIPSETT.
Boston : Roberts Bros.

KING (MAUDE EGERTON).
ROUND ABOUT A BRIGHTON COACH OFFICE. With 30 Illustrations by LUCY KEMP WELCH. Cr. 8vo. 5s. net. [*In preparation.*

LANDER (HARRY).
WEIGHED IN THE BALANCE : A Novel. Crown 8vo. 4s. 6d. net. [*In preparation.*

LANG (ANDREW). *See* STODDART.

LEATHER (R. K.).
VERSES. 250 copies. Fcap. 8vo. 3s. net.
Transferred by the Author to the present Publisher.

LE GALLIENNE (RICHARD).
PROSE FANCIES. With Portrait of the Author by WILSON STEER. Fourth Edition. Crown 8vo. Purple cloth. 5s. net.
Also a limited large paper edition. 12s. 6d. net.
New York : G. P. Putnam's Sons.
THE BOOK BILLS OF NARCISSUS, An Account rendered by RICHARD LE GALLIENNE. Third Edition. With a Frontispiece. Crown 8vo. Purple cloth. 3s. 6d. net.
Also 50 copies on large paper. 8vo. 10s. 6d. net.
New York : G. P. Putman's Sons.
ROBERT LOUIS STEVENSON, AN ELEGY, AND OTHER POEMS, MAINLY PERSONAL. With Etched Title-page by D. Y. CAMERON. Cr. 8vo. Purple cloth. 4s. 6d. net.
Also 75 copies on large paper. 8vo. 12s. 6d. net.
Boston : Copeland & Day.
ENGLISH POEMS. Fourth Edition, revised. Crown 8vo. Purple cloth. 4s. 6d. net.
Boston : Copeland & Day.

LE GALLIENNE (RICHARD).

RETROSPECTIVE REVIEWS, A LITERARY LOG, 1891-1895. 2 vols. crown 8vo. Purple cloth. 9s. net.
[In preparation.
New York: Dodd, Mead & Co.

GEORGE MEREDITH: Some Characteristics. With a Bibliography (much enlarged) by JOHN LANE, Portrait, etc. Fourth Edition. Cr. 8vo. Purple cloth. 5s. 6d. net.

THE RELIGION OF A LITERARY MAN. 5th thousand. Crown 8vo. Purple cloth. 3s. 6d. net.

Also a special rubricated edition on hand-made paper. 8vo. 10s. 6d. net.

New York: G. P. Putnam's Sons.

LIPSETT (CALDWELL).

ORANGE AND GREEN. (*See* KEYNOTES SERIES.)

LOWRY (H. D.).

WOMEN'S TRAGEDIES. (*See* KEYNOTES SERIES.)

LUCAS (WINIFRED).

A VOLUME OF POEMS. Fcap. 8vo. 4s. 6d. net.
[In preparation.

LYNCH (HANNAH).

THE GREAT GALEOTO AND FOLLY OR SAINTLINESS. Two Plays, from the Spanish of JOSÉ ECHEGARAY, with an Introduction. Small 4to. 5s. 6d. net.
Boston: Lamson, Wolffe & Co.

MACHEN (ARTHUR).

THE GREAT GOD PAN. (*See* KEYNOTES SERIES.)
THE THREE IMPOSTORS. (*See* KEYNOTES SERIES.)

MACLEOD (FIONA).

THE MOUNTAIN LOVERS. (*See* KEYNOTES SERIES.)

MAKOWER (STANLEY V.).

THE MIRROR OF MUSIC. (*See* KEYNOTES SERIES.)

MARZIALS (THEO.).

THE GALLERY OF PIGEONS AND OTHER POEMS. Post 8vo. 4s. 6d. net.   *[Very few remain.*
Transferred by the Author to the present Publisher.

MATHEW (FRANK).

THE WOOD OF THE BRAMBLES: A Novel. Crown 8vo. 4s. 6d. net.   *[In preparation.*

THE MAYFAIR SET.
> Each volume fcap. 8vo.   3s. 6d. net.
> Vol. I. THE AUTOBIOGRAPHY OF A BOY: Passages selected by his Friend, G. S. STREET.   With a Title-page designed by C. W. FURSE.
>> [*Fourth Edition now ready.*
> Vol. II. THE JONESES AND THE ASTERISKS: a Story in Monologue.   By GERALD CAMPBELL.   With Title-page and six Illustrations by F. H. TOWNSEND.
> Vol. III. SELECT CONVERSATIONS WITH AN UNCLE NOW EXTINCT.   By H. G. WELLS.   With Title-page by F. H. TOWNSEND.
>> *The following are in preparation.*
> Vol. IV. THE FEASTS OF AUTOLYCUS: The Diary of a Greedy Woman.   Edited by ELIZABETH ROBINS PENNELL.
> Vol. V. MRS ALBERT GRUNDY: Observations in Philistia. By HAROLD FREDERIC.
> Vol. VI. FOR PLAIN WOMEN ONLY.   By GEORGE FLEMING.
>> New York : The Merriam Company.

MEREDITH (GEORGE).
> THE FIRST PUBLISHED PORTRAIT OF THIS AUTHOR, engraved on the wood by W. BISCOMBE GARDNER, after the painting by G. F. WATTS.   Proof copies on Japanese vellum, signed by painter and engraver. £1, 1s. net.

MEYNELL (MRS.), (ALICE C. THOMPSON).
> POEMS.   Fcap. 8vo.   3s. 6d. net.   [*Out of Print at present.*
> A few of the 50 large paper copies (First Edition) remain, 12s. 6d. net.
> THE RHYTHM OF LIFE AND OTHER ESSAYS.   Second Edition.   Fcap. 8vo.   3s. 6d. net.
> A few of the 50 large paper copies (First Edition) remain, 12s. 6d. net.
> *See also* HAKE.

MILLER (JOAQUIN).
> THE BUILDING OF THE CITY BEAUTIFUL.   Fcap. 8vo. With a Decorated Cover.   5s. net.
>> Chicago : Stone & Kimball.

MILMAN (LENA).
> DOSTOIEVSKY'S POOR FOLK.   (*See* KEYNOTES SERIES.)

MONKHOUSE (ALLAN).

BOOKS AND PLAYS : A Volume of Essays on Meredith, Borrow, Ibsen, and others. 400 copies. Crown 8vo. 5s. net.

Philadelphia : J. B. Lippincott Co.

MOORE (GEORGE).

See KEYNOTES SERIES, Vol. III.

NESBIT (E.).

A POMANDER OF VERSE. With a Title-page and Cover designed by LAURENCE HOUSMAN. Crown 8vo. 5s. net.

Chicago : A. C. McClurg & Co.

IN HOMESPUN. (*See* KEYNOTES SERIES.)

NETTLESHIP (J. T.).

ROBERT BROWNING : Essays and Thoughts. Third Edition. With a Portrait. Crown 8vo. 5s. 6d. net.

New York : Chas. Scribner's Sons.

NOBLE (JAS. ASHCROFT).

THE SONNET IN ENGLAND AND OTHER ESSAYS. Title-page and Cover Design by AUSTIN YOUNG. 600 copies. Crown 8vo. 5s. net.

Also 50 copies large paper. 12s. 6d. net.

O'SHAUGHNESSY (ARTHUR).

HIS LIFE AND HIS WORK. With Selections from his Poems. By LOUISE CHANDLER MOULTON. Portrait and Cover Design. Fcap. 8vo. 5s. net.

Chicago : Stone & Kimball.

OXFORD CHARACTERS.

A series of lithographed portraits by WILL ROTHENSTEIN, with text by F. YORK POWELL and others. To be issued monthly in term. Each number will contain two portraits. Parts I. to VI. ready. 200 sets only, folio, wrapper, 5s. net per part; 25 special large paper sets containing proof impressions of the portraits signed by the artist, 10s. 6d. net per part.

PENNELL (ELIZABETH ROBINS).

THE FEASTS OF AUTOLYCUS. (*See* MAYFAIR SET.)

PETERS (WM. THEODORE).

POSIES OUT OF RINGS. Sq. 16mo. 3s. 6d. net.

[*In preparation.*

PIERROT'S LIBRARY.
Each volume with Title-page, Cover Design, and End-papers designed by AUBREY BEARDSLEY. Sq. 16mo. 2s. 6d. net.
The following are in preparation.
Vol. I. PIERROT. By H. DE VERE STACPOOLE.
Vol. II. MY LITTLE LADY ANNE. By Mrs EGERTON CASTLE.
Vol. III. DEATH, THE KNIGHT AND THE LADY. By H. DE VERE STACPOOLE.
Vol. IV. SIMPLICITY. By A. T. G. PRICE.
Philadelphia : Henry Altemus.

PISSARRO (LUCIEN).
THE QUEEN OF THE FISHES. A Story of the Valois, adapted by MARGARET RUST, being a printed manuscript, decorated with pictures and other ornaments, cut on the wood by LUCIEN PISSARO, and printed by him in divers colours and in gold at his press in Epping. Edition limited to 70 copies, each numbered and signed. Crown 8vo, on Japanese hand-made paper, bound in vellum, £1 net.

PLARR (VICTOR).
IN THE DORIAN MOOD : Poems. Crown 8vo. 5s. net.
[*In preparation.*

PRICE (A. T. G.).
SIMPLICITY. (*See* PIERROT'S LIBRARY.)

RADFORD (DOLLIE).
SONGS AND OTHER VERSES. With Title-page designed by PATTEN WILSON. Fcap. 8vo. 4s. 6d. net.
Philadelphia : J. B. Lippincott Co.

RAMSDEN (HERMIONE).
See HANSSON.

RICKETTS (C. S.) AND C. H. SHANNON.
HERO AND LEANDER. By CHRISTOPHER MARLOWE and GEORGE CHAPMAN. With Borders, Initials, and Illustrations designed and engraved on the wood by C. S. RICKETTS and C. H. SHANNON. Bound in English vellum and gold. 200 copies only. 35s. net.
Boston : Copeland & Day.

RHYS (ERNEST).
A LONDON ROSE AND OTHER RHYMES. With Title-page designed by SELWYN IMAGE. 350 copies. Crown 8vo. 5s. net.
New York : Dodd, Mead & Co.

ROBERTSON (JOHN M.).
ESSAYS TOWARDS A CRITICAL METHOD. (New Series.)
Crown 8vo. 5s. net. [*In preparation.*

ROBINSON (C. NEWTON).
THE VIOL OF LOVE. With Ornaments and Cover Design
by LAURENCE HOUSMAN. Crown 8vo. 5s. net.
Boston : Lamson, Wolffe & Co.

ST. CYRES (LORD).
THE LITTLE FLOWERS OF ST. FRANCIS: A new ren-
dering into English of the Fioretti di San Francesco.
Crown 8vo. 5s. net. [*In preparation.*

SHARP (EVELYN).
AT THE RELTON ARMS. (*See* KEYNOTES SERIES.)

SHIEL (M. P.).
PRINCE ZALESKI. (*See* KEYNOTES SERIES.)

SMITH (JOHN).
PLATONIC AFFECTIONS. (*See* KEYNOTES SERIES.)

STACPOOLE (H. DE VERE).
PIERROT. (*See* PIERROT'S LIBRARY.)
DEATH, THE KNIGHT AND THE LADY. (*See* PIERROT'S
LIBRARY).

STEVENSON (ROBERT LOUIS).
PRINCE OTTO. A rendering in French by EGERTON
CASTLE. Crown 8vo. 5s. net. [*In preparation.*
Also 100 copies on large paper, uniform in size with the Edinburgh
Edition of the Works.
A CHILD'S GARDEN OF VERSES. With nearly 100
Illustrations by CHARLES ROBINSON. Crown 8vo.
5s. net. [*In preparation.*

STODDART (THOS. TOD).
THE DEATH WAKE. With an Introduction by ANDREW
LANG. Fcap. 8vo. 5s. net.
Chicago : Way & Williams.

STREET (G. S.).
THE AUTOBIOGRAPHY OF A BOY. (*See* MAYFAIR SET.)
MINIATURES AND MOODS. Fcap. 8vo. 3s. net.
Transferred by the Author to the present Publisher.
New York : The Merriam Co.

SWETTENHAM (F. A.).
MALAY SKETCHES. With Title-page and Cover Design
by PATTEN WILSON. Crown 8vo. 5s. net.
New York : Macmillan & Co.

SYRETT (NETTA).
NOBODY'S FAULT. (*See* KEYNOTES SERIES.)

TABB (JOHN B.).
POEMS. Sq. 32mo. 4s. 6d. net.
Boston: Copeland & Day.

TAYLOR (UNA).
NETS FOR THE WIND. (*See* KEYNOTES SERIES.)

TENNYSON (FREDERICK).
POEMS OF THE DAY AND YEAR. With a Title-page by
PATTEN WILSON. Crown 8vo. 5s. net.
Chicago: Stone & Kimball.

THIMM (C. A.).
A COMPLETE BIBLIOGRAPHY OF THE ART OF FENCE,
DUELLING, ETC. With Illustrations. [*In preparation.*

THOMPSON (FRANCIS).
POEMS. With Frontispiece, Title-page, and Cover Design
by LAURENCE HOUSMAN. Fourth Edition. Pott
4to. 5s. net.
Boston: Copeland & Day.
SISTER SONGS: An Offering to Two Sisters. With Frontis-
piece, Title-page, and Cover Design by LAURENCE
HOUSMAN. Pott 4to. 5s. net.
Boston: Copeland & Day.

THOREAU (HENRY DAVID).
POEMS OF NATURE. Selected and edited by HENRY S.
SALT and FRANK B. SANBORN, with a Title-page
designed by PATTEN WILSON. Fcap. 8vo. 4s. 6d.
net. [*In preparation.*
Boston and New York: Houghton, Mifflin & Co.

TYNAN HINKSON (KATHARINE).
CUCKOO SONGS. With Title-page and Cover Design by
LAURENCE HOUSMAN. Fcap. 8vo. 5s. net.
Boston: Copeland & Day.
MIRACLE PLAYS: OUR LORD'S COMING AND CHILDHOOD.
With Six Illustrations and a Title-page by PATTEN
WILSON. Fcap. 8vo. net. [*In preparation.*
Chicago: Stone & Kimball.

WATSON (ROSAMUND MARRIOTT).
VESPERTILIA AND OTHER POEMS. With a Title-page
designed by R. ANNING BELL. Fcap. 8vo. 4s. 6d.
net.
A SUMMER NIGHT AND OTHER POEMS. New edition,
with a decorative Title-page. Fcap. 8vo. 3s. net.
Chicago: Way & Williams. [*In preparation.*

WATSON (H. B. MARRIOTT).
AT THE FIRST CORNER. (*See* KEYNOTES SERIES.)
THE KING'S HIGHWAY. Crown 8vo. 4s. 6d. net.
[*In preparation.*

WATSON (WILLIAM).

ODES AND OTHER POEMS. Fourth Edition. Fcap. 8vo,
buckram. 4s. 6d. net.
New York : Macmillan & Co.
THE ELOPING ANGELS : A Caprice. Second Edition.
Square 16mo, buckram. 3s. 6d. net.
New York : Macmillan & Co.
EXCURSIONS IN CRITICISM : being some Prose Recrea-
tions of a Rhymer. Second Edition. Cr. 8vo. 5s. net.
New York : Macmillan & Co.
THE PRINCE'S QUEST AND OTHER POEMS. With a
Bibliographical Note added. Second Edition. Fcap.
8vo. 4s. 6d. net.

WATT (FRANCIS).

THE LAW'S LUMBER ROOM. Fcap. 8vo. 3s. 6d. net.
Chicago : A. C. McClurg & Co.

WATTS (THEODORE).

POEMS. Crown 8vo. 5s. net.   [*In preparation.*
There will also be an Edition de Luxe *of this volume printed at
the Kelmscott Press.*

WELLS (H. G.).

SELECT CONVERSATIONS WITH AN UNCLE. (*See* MAY-
FAIR SET.)

WHARTON (H. T.).

SAPPHO. Memoir, Text, Selected Renderings, and a
Literal Translation by HENRY THORNTON WHARTON.
With three Illustrations in Photogravure, and a Cover
designed by AUBREY BEARDSLEY. Fcap. 8vo.
7s. 6d. net.
Chicago : A. C. McClurg & Co.

THE YELLOW BOOK

An Illustrated Quarterly

Pott 4to. 5s. net.

VOLUME I.   April 1894. 272 pages. 15 Illustrations.
[*Out of print.*
VOLUME II.   July 1894. 364 pages. 23 Illustrations.
VOLUME III.   October 1894. 280 pages. 15 Illustrations.
VOLUME IV.   January 1895. 285 pages. 16 Illustrations.
VOLUME V.   April 1895. 317 pages. 14 Illustrations.
VOLUME VI.   July 1895. 335 pages. 16 Illustrations.
Boston : Copeland & Day.